Simon the Cat
Earns His Wings
Bogey Arrives
The Story Of Two Special Kitties

Margaret Rose Erickson
Lisa Joan Fruscella

www.simonthecat.ca

Tellwell Talent
www.tellwell.ca

ISBN
978-0-2288-5403-6 (Hardcover)
978-0-2288-5402-9 (Paperback)

PREFACE

Unlike the prior three books, this book was written after our beloved Simon the Cat crossed the Rainbow Bridge and is in Animal Heaven.

As Simon looks down from his lofty heights, he sees a tiny orange kitty lost and alone in the forest. He can also see that his earthly mom and dad are very unhappy. They miss him so very much and seem to cry a great deal of the time.

Simon decides to do something about the situation, read on to see just how wonderfully well Simon the Cat comes to the rescue!

The book is in two parts:

SIMON'S STORY

BOGEY'S STORY

It is the intent of the book to help children, as well as adults, cope with the loss of a pet and perhaps realize another pet may be just around the corner, lost and alone, waiting to be adopted and loved.

We so hope you enjoy reading this book as much as we have enjoyed writing it. Both the Humane Society and the SPCA/ASPCA will receive funds from the sale proceeds of the book.

Margaret Rose Erickson - Lisa Joan Fruscella
co-authors and mother/daughter

www.simonthecat.ca

AUTHORS' NOTES

Simon the Cat was rescued when he was 2 years old and lived until he was 15. He seemed to know from day 1 he was rescued and bestowed more love than one could imagine. He was the subject of three prior books, travelled over 80,000 miles in the back seat of a truck, had 3 t.v. appearances and made money for the Humane Society and the SPCA/ASPCA from his t.v. appearances and books. When Simon crossed the Rainbow Bridge in February of 2020, we thought we could never love another kitty. The void in our hearts was huge.

Then one day while golfing, a small orange kitten, obviously lost, starving and afraid, appeared on the golf cart path. We left the kitten there, even though he ran after our cart. Ashamed that we had left him, we went back some time later, searched and searched, to no avail. The next day while the 'dad' in this book was golfing, the little orange kitty ran up to his cart. The rest is history. We brought him home, fed him and he is now the love of our life. This part of the book is factual. From that experience this book was born.

We truly believe there was intervention by our Simon the Cat to send us the little orange kitty. Bogey (the name we chose as it is a golf term) has snuggled his way into our hearts and is an absolute delight. He was found in October, 2020 and weighed 4 lbs. In April of 2021 he weighs 14 lbs. and is still growing. He loves life and we love him.

The book was written not only to help cope with the loss of a pet but also hoping readers will open their hearts and their homes to homeless animals. DON'T SHOP FOR PETS ADOPT.

M.R. and Lisa

Bogey the Cat – Day 1

Simon the Cat

DEDICATION

This book is dedicated to the memory of two special pets – SIMON THE CAT and COBY THE DOG. There is a famous saying "it is better to have loved and lost, than never to have loved at all" – well truer words could never be spoken when it comes to loving our pets. Simon and Coby required so little and gave so much.

When our pets cross over the Rainbow Bridge - we grieve - then we have sweet memories – which last forever.

Our SIMON THE CAT is described on the previous page – no more is required. He was one in a million.

As to COBY THE DOG, no dog could be loved more or return that love more, than this beautiful, intelligent, lovable chocolate lab. Both Margaret Rose and Lisa remember planting a huge garden, had it all done, when Coby came rushing through the fields to greet Lisa, managing to hit every row of planted seeds. That year we had corn in with peas, carrots in with beans, radish in with lettuce and Coby in our hearts. David Champion (MR's nephew, Lisa's cousin) this little write up is for you and in memory of your COBY.

Simon the Cat

Coby the Dog

Coby and Lisa

David and Simon

SIMON'S STORY

Simon woke after a very long nap thinking how he had slept the entire morning away and was still so very tired. Simon's mom came into the room and hugged Simon ever so tight. "Simon my love, you have a warm nose and do not look very well, I think we should take you to the Vet."

Simon thought, "Oh, I love every single person at the Vet, I don't mind going there at all. I am not feeling very well that's for sure."

Simon's Dad wrapped him in his warm, comfy white blanket and off they went to the Vet.

Doctor Carling saw Simon right away and knew immediately that he was not well. She checked him over very thoroughly. When Doctor Carling had completed all her tests, she told Simon's mom and dad, with tears in her eyes, that Simon was indeed very ill and could not get better.

Simon's mom and dad took him home and spent all the rest of that day and night loving and cuddling him. Simon was too tired to even smile so he curled up in between his mom and dad in their big bed and went sound asleep.

The next morning Dr. Carling came to see Simon who was being cuddled in his dad's arms in his warm, snuggly white blanket. Doctor Carling put her arms around Simon and gave him a loving pet on his head. She then gave Simon some very special medicine. Simon's last thought was, "Oh my goodness I feel so much better and I think I am leaving to go somewhere, oh my goodness!"

At that very moment Simon had left his earthly home and his spirit was soaring to the sky.

"Oh my goodness," Simon said out loud, "I am high in the air. I just went over a beautiful Rainbow Bridge. I am in the clouds. I am being cuddled by the clouds."

Every cloud that floated by was soft and fluffy and every sunbeam that tickled his face made him want to smile. He was so content. Truly this was a wonderful place.

Suddenly a very large cat appeared before him. "Wow," thought Simon, "what a big kitty and she has such a beautiful face and WINGS!"

"Simon you are now in Animal Heaven. This is a place where you will live forever with all of your friends who have gone before you and many more yet to come. You have been a very good kitty and now you have earned your wings."

"Oh, my goodness," thought Simon, "what is that on my back, why it is wings, I can fly."

Simon just had to test his wings and gave a big, happy meow as he flew around from cloud to cloud. He flew very slowly as this was all so new to him. Soon a group of kitties surrounded him, all with wings. He could hear kitties calling him from all sides. "Hi Simon, come fly with us," yelled Ralph and Buttons. "Over here with us," called Squeak, Cheechoo and Gatito. "You will like this bouncy cloud," said George, Sammy, Benny and Jade. There were kitties everywhere all wanting to be friends with Simon, hundreds of them it seemed. Simon tested his wings again and sure enough he was able to follow all his newly made friends. Soon they were flying over beautiful fields filled with flowers and butterflies and kitties were jumping up and down and playing, what a great time they were having. Simon waved his paws and did somersaults in the air. He was so happy.

Just when he thought he had seen everything and was bubbling over with excitement, Cheechoo said, "You have to see where all the friendly dogs are playing. There are also rabbits, turtles, guinea pigs and hamsters, lots of birds and so many more animals you cannot imagine. You see Simon this is Animal Heaven and we all get along and love one another." "Oh my goodness," thought Simon, "I think I am going to cry those happy tears again."

"Look down Simon," said Cheechoo, "they are so happy, you see this is a very special day, for today they get their wings." "Wow." thought Simon, "soon they will be flying around with me, I can hardly wait."

Ralph and Buttons, who were brothers, reminded Simon that they had also lived with his mom and dad a long time ago. Buttons told him that when Ralph crossed the Rainbow Bridge his mom and dad moved and he went to live with a wonderful lady called Kathy who was his mom number 2. She loved him very much just like he loved her. Simon was so happy to hear about Ralph and Buttons that he just had to do another summersault and meowed at the top of his lungs. As he was doing this, another kitty called to him, "Hi Simon, my name is Benny and our earthly moms are really good friends – did you know that?" Simon thought for a minute and then he remembered that a very kind lady named Patty often visited his mom and dad and always played with him. That was Benny's mom and Simon once more meowed loudly and happily.

Sammy, George, Squeak, Gatito and Jade were playing hopscotch on clouds. Simon thought he would love to play that game, it really looked like fun. Animal Heaven was certainly a wonderful place to be.

The kitties all started to swoop down towards where the dogs were having a game of chase. The first dogs Simon saw were Coby, Maddy, Keira and Jumbo. Then he saw Randy, Rudy and Mac. They called up to Simon, waving their paws, "Hi Simon, welcome, welcome, we are so glad to see you, come over to our playground any time. We love to jump in the air and chase butterflies, just like you. The butterflies laugh with us and land on our noses, bet you would like that." "Indeed I would," thought Simon. As Simon looked at all the animals having such a wonderful time, he knew that having wings and flying everywhere was the most wonderful feeling in the whole wide world.

Simon noticed a pig go flying by. Simon remembered his mom saying "that will be the day when pigs fly" and he thought to himself "pigs really CAN and DO fly." He laughed and laughed over that.

Maddy and Coby came rushing over to Simon. Maddy said "I remember when my earthly mom and dad were so sad when I earned my wings. They cried a lot but did adopt another little puppy who really needed a home, her name is Lucy, and they are very happy. They still love me but they made room in their hearts for Lucy." Coby said, "Simon, every day I look down on David. He sometimes feels my presence and that is when I am sending him a whole lot of love. I think he knows I earned my wings and am very happy." This made Simon think long and hard on how he could make his earthly mom and dad feel better.

One day when Simon and a few of his friends were playing 'cloud jump', Simon looked way down on earth and could see his mom and dad were very sad and were crying for him. He listened very closely and could hear his mom say to his dad, "I miss our Simon so much." "Hmm," thought Simon, "I wonder what I can do about that," as he remembered Maddy's story and Coby's words. Just then Simon spotted a tiny orange coloured kitten lost in a forest near the golf course where his mom and dad played golf. "I know just what I can do about that!" Simon said.

His spirt soared down to earth and whispered in the little kitty's ear, "Do not be afraid little kitty, my name is Simon and I am a kitty just like you, go out on the cart path, I think someone will see you and be very kind to you."

The little kitty thought, "I think I felt the fluttering of wings and heard a whisper in my ear, I will do what the voice said."

He went out to the cart path just as a golf cart was pulling away with a mom and a dad in the cart. He ran after the cart meowing but the cart left and he was all alone again. He went back into the forest crying and so wishing they had stopped.

Once more the little orange kitty knew he was all alone in the forest. His first memories were being with his brothers in a barn, curled up against their furry mom. One day he saw a mouse and chased the mouse right out of the barn and into a field. "Aha!" he thought, "Wait until mom and all my brothers see what I can do. I will bring this mouse home to the barn." The mouse was very fast and ran a very long distance, zigzagging through the field. The little orange kitten lost him and even worse lost his way home! "Whatever shall I do," he thought, "I am really frightened and also very hungry and cold." He curled up in a tight little ball under a tree.

Every so often he would peek out from behind a tree and see golfers going by in their carts. Sometimes they dropped bits of food on the ground and he would run quickly to eat it up. Then he would go back under the tree and try his best to keep safe and warm.

What the little orange kitty did not know, was that it was Simon's mom and dad in the cart that drove away. Simon's mom said, "We should have brought food for that little kitty, what if he didn't have a home." They got him food and went back but he was gone. They searched and searched but could not find him. The little orange kitty was back under his tree trying to keep warm and feeling very sad. He finally fell asleep, cold, hungry and alone.

The next morning just as he was waking, he again heard the whisper in his ear and he was sure he felt the fluttering of wings. The voice told him to go back to the cart path and wait, someone would find him.

"Gosh", he thought, "I'm a little frightened to go out there again but I do see a golf cart and the same man from yesterday is in it." He went slowly to the cart and the man quickly picked him up, gave him some water and food and took him home. It was Simon's dad and now the little orange kitty was safe and warm.

Simon's mom looked at the kitty and said, "Let's feed him and make him welcome and I think we should give him a name." Now one of the names used in golf is "Bogey" and that was the name they gave the little orange kitty.

Simon's dad had stored all of Simon's favourite toys and now was so happy he had done so. He also found a kitty bed and kitty trees. He showed the bed to Bogey. Bogey did not know what it was but he did know it was warm and now that he had a full tummy he was very tired so he curled up in the kitty bed and went fast asleep.

Simon looked down from a cloud where he had been playing and saw what had happened. "Oh my goodness, how happy I feel," he thought, "my mom and dad are smiling again and that little kitty has a new home. I will now enjoy my new life and know that Bogey will too." With that Simon was off to play with his friends, a huge smile on his face.

BOGEY'S STORY

Bogey opened his eyes and looked around. "Where am I," he thought. Then he remembered how a kind man had brought him to this house where a kind lady fed him and put him in this warm snuggly bed. "Oh gosh," he thought, "I have never been in a house before, I don't know what to do." He jumped out of his bed and walked slowly around the room looking at everything. He saw a tree house for kitties, kitty toys on the floor and soft blankets everywhere.

Bogey thought, "It is so nice and warm here, I wonder if I will be allowed to stay. I better not get my hopes up for they may return me to the forest. I hope not!"

Just then the kind lady and man came into the room. The lady said, "Bogey dear, you can now live with us, this is your forever home and we are now your mom and dad." Bogey could hardly believe his ears. He would never have to go back to the forest, he would never be alone and cold and hungry again. Little tears ran down his cheeks he was so happy. Bogey did not know this, but another kitty named Simon used to live here and he often cried happy tears as well.

Bogey's mom then showed him all over the house. Soon he knew where everything was including his own kitty dishes which were filled with food.

He did get one fright when his mom turned on the wall television. He thought there were people in the wall and he jumped high in the air in fear. His mom just laughed and said, "Bogey dear, that is called a television and you are just seeing pictures, they are not here at all." Bogey smiled and thought how silly he was. He didn't know it then but soon he would love to watch t.v., particularly golf and hockey games.

Out a patio door was a huge deck. Bogey looked up at his mom who said, "Let's go out on the deck in the fresh air, maybe you will see some neighbours." Sure enough, as soon as Bogey ran out on the deck, Abby the neighbour dog sent him a "woof woof" and waved her paw. Bogey meowed back and waved his paw. Already he had made a new friend.

They went back inside and Bogey's mom showed him how to get up in his kitty trees and also showed him all his toys. "Oh my," he thought, "I think I am the luckiest kitty in the whole wide world."

BOGEY   **ABBY**

Bogey ate his breakfast all up and loved the feeling of a very full tummy. His mom told him they would now be going to the Vet to be sure he was a healthy little kitty. Bogey did not know what a Vet was but he knew that if his mom and dad wanted him to see the Vet, then he would be safe, so he happily looked forward to this new adventure.

Bogey jumped into his little kitty carrier and they were off to see the Vet. Bogey was introduced to all the girls at the front desk in the Vet's office. They all talked to him and told him what a fine kitty he was. "I like it here," he thought.

He then went into a special kitty room where he saw Dr. Morgan. She was very gentle and checked him all over. She even gave him a little hug which made Bogey look up at her with a big smile on his face. "Bogey you are a bit under weight, we will give you some special food so you will grow strong and healthy." She was so nice Bogey purred in contentment. He loved going to the Vet and he loved Dr. Morgan.

On the drive home Bogey looked out the car window and jumped up and down with excitement. There was so much to see, playgrounds, kids, cars, parks, he could not believe his eyes. Bogey had never ventured out of the forest so everything he saw was brand new to him. He loved watching the children play, it looked like so much fun. He saw teeter totters, merry go rounds, ball fields and slides. "Wow," he thought, "this must be the best place in the whole world to live."

His mom and dad laughed as they saw how excited Bogey was becoming and realized their little Bogey was only months old and had never experienced living anywhere except in a barn and in the forest. They decided then and there to take him to lots of places so he could see just how beautiful the world could be.

Bogey saw they were turning into his yard and his house, he just loved being able to think, "this is now my yard and my house too." He was jumping up and down with excitement to get inside to see his toys, his tree house and his lovely little kitty bed. Bogey spent the rest of the day having so much fun. He ran from room to room exploring. He was a little afraid of stairs but after a few tries he was running up and down as fast as the wind. He found he had his very own little kitty door leading out to the deck so he ran outside and waved at Abby. Life was wonderful for little Bogey.

Bogey heard CLICK CLICK and wondered what mom and dad were doing. They were standing on each end of a long, narrow table throwing little blue and red rocks back and forth. "Bogey, would you like to play?" his mom asked. "Oh yes," thought Bogey and jumped up on the table. He immediately went sliding all the way down the table, it was very slippery. His dad laughed and said, "Bogey, this is a shuffleboard and there is wax on the surface. It makes the rocks slide along very quickly but I guess it makes little kitties slide along very quickly as well." Bogey chased the rocks back and forth from one end to the other sliding all the way. "Whee, this is fun", he thought, "I love shuffleboard."

From that time on Bogey always tried to get his mom and dad down to the games room to play shuffleboard. He would meow at them and then go dashing downstairs and jump up on the shuffleboard. His mom and dad would laugh and play with him every single day. Sometimes he would get very tired and then just lie down right in the middle and catch the rocks with his little paws. This made his mom and dad laugh even more.

BOGEY PLAYS SHUFFLEBOARD

BOGEY ASLEEP ON SHUFFLEBOARD

Bogey woke up to great excitement going on in his house. "Oh goodness," he thought, "mom and dad are bringing in a tree from the forest, it looks just like the tree where I used to hide. I wonder what they are doing." He looked at his mom and dad with a funny little expression on his kitty face. "Why Bogey dear, of course you would not know about Christmas trees. You see this is a very wonderful time of the year for celebration. We celebrate the birth of a very special baby named Jesus, we decorate a tree and we put presents under the tree. On Christmas morning which is December 25th, we open the presents." "Gosh," thought Bogey, "that should be fun."

The next day was even more exciting. "Oh goodness," he thought, I wonder what is happening with the special tree." He watched his mom and dad decorate the tree and it grew more beautiful every minute. "It certainly does not look like the trees in the forest now," he thought. Then he saw all the presents under the tree and it seemed every one of them had his name on it. He had to hold back those happy tears again.

That night before he went to bed, Bogey sat and stared at the beautiful Christmas tree. It was now covered with lights and ornaments and at the very top was a lovely white angel. He sat for a very long time and just could not believe a tree could be that beautiful.

It was very late at night, Bogey's mom and dad were fast asleep, but Bogey could not sleep. He just had to look at the tree once more. "I think it would be alright if I climbed up in the tree to have a closer look at the angel," he thought. Using the string of lights for his paws to give him balance, little Bogey began climbing the tree to get to the very top where he could really see the angel. One of his back legs got stuck in a light cord. "Oh, oh," thought Bogey, I will just flip around and get unstuck!" But then his front legs got stuck in the lights and he twisted until he was upside down, all tangled up, with just his little face peering out from the branches. "Oh, no," thought Bogey, "and I was almost to the top." Just then he was sure he felt the fluttering of wings and a voice in his ear saying "just be very still, you will soon be free." He gave a little 'MEEOW' and stayed very still. At the same time Bogey's mom and dad woke up. His mom said "I had the strangest dream about Simon, he was telling me Bogey needed us." Bogey's mom and dad now heard the MEEOW for real and ran to the Christmas tree where they found little Bogey looking eagerly towards them. Bogey's dad quickly untangled his little legs and put him in his mom's arms. Bogey purred happily as his mom gave him a big hug.

His dad then put tape all around the wires of the tree and taped them to the inner branches so they would never again be loose enough to trap a little kitty's legs. Bogey was so happy to be free and his legs really didn't hurt at all. He decided he would never climb a Christmas tree again as he cuddled close to his mom and dad. He heard his dad say they also learned a valuable lesson and would never leave loose wires hanging on a Christmas tree again.

One morning Bogey heard his mom on the telephone, laughing and talking excitedly. After she hung up, she cuddled Bogey and said, "your sister is coming to visit." Sister? Bogey did not know he had a sister. "She is my daughter and is coming to visit from New York. We are picking her up from the airport tomorrow."

"What is an airport?" Bogey thought to himself, "and what is New York?" Bogey hoped his sister would be fluffy and a bit smaller than himself (he liked to think he would make a good big brother) and that she liked to play. The next day Bogey watched from the window as his mom and dad left for the airport. He could hardly wait for them to return with this sister of his.

It seemed like no time at all when the door opened and his mom and dad were home. Behind them another person ran into the living room, dropped to her knees, and with her arms out, cried, "Oh Bogey! I am so glad to meet you. I am your sister Lisa." Bogey ran under the couch and hid. This was his sister? She was awfully big and loud, plus, she did not have fur or paws!

Lisa waited patiently and soon Bogey poked his little head out from the couch and timidly walked up to her. She put her arms around him and gave him a big hug. "Oh my," he thought, "she really is very nice, I think I do like her." Soon they were rolling on the floor laughing and having a great time. Having a sister just like Lisa was lots of fun.

The next day Lisa asked Bogey if he would like to go outside for a walk. Bogey's mom and dad had bought him a harness and a leash, so they could walk outside together without Bogey wandering off and getting lost, as he was known to do. "Okay," thought Bogey, "she is my sister, so I will go for a walk with her." Off they went, strolling down the neighborhood streets.

Bogey was a tiny bit nervous, being away from his mom and dad, but was very much enjoying walking along with his sister. Suddenly a big dog came running down the sidewalk in front of them, pulling on his leash. "Yikes!" thought Bogey, "this dog is scary!" and he decided to climb up Lisa's leg to get away from him. "YOUCH" cried Lisa, as Bogey's little nails gripped and scrambled up her leg. "YEEEOUCH" she cried again, as Bogey climbed right up to the top of her head, and dug his nails in to her hair so he would not fall.

"Hang on, Bogey!" Lisa cried, and stuck her hands up over her head to steady him, "I'm taking you home!" and they raced down the street together, harness and leash left far behind as they scurried away. They arrived safely home and collapsed on the front steps. They then began to laugh and laugh and laugh. Bogey thought, "Wow my sister really protected me and we did look very funny." Bogey's mom and dad came out to see what all the ruckus was about. When they heard about their amazing adventure they laughed as well and could only imagine what Bogey looked like on top of Lisa's head.

The house was very quiet. Bogey's mom and dad were sound asleep in their bed and his sister, Lisa, had left that afternoon to return to New York.

For some reason Bogey could not sleep so he wandered from room to room looking at his kitty trees and all his toys.

"I am so lucky," he thought, "I love my new forever home and my family."

As he stretched out on his kitty bed, he suddenly remembered his time in the forest when he was lost and alone. He also remembered the voice he heard in his ear and the flutter of wings. "I wonder who was helping me," he thought, as he drifted off to sleep.

At that exact moment there was a flutter of wings and a voice again whispered in his ear.

The voice said, "Goodnight little Bogey, you are safe and happy now. My work is indeed done so I will no longer need to guide you. I will return to my heavenly home where I am also safe and happy. Your friend, SIMON THE CAT."

Little Bogey was fast asleep but stirred when he heard Simon's words. He remembered that voice and purred contentedly as he now understood how he had come to be here in his forever home. He sleepily smiled and said, "THANK YOU SIMON THE CAT."

SIMON THE CAT

BOGEY THE CAT

TO OUR WONDERFUL VETERINARIANS AT CENTRAL VETERINARY CLINIC IN PONOKA - WE THANK YOU NOT ONLY FOR YOUR PROFESSIONALISM BUT YOUR SINCERE LOVE OF OUR PETS. DOCTOR CARLING, YOUR COMPASSION AT THE TIME YOU CAME TO OUR HOME AND HELPED OUR SIMON THE CAT CROSS OVER THE RAINBOW BRIDGE WILL BE REMEMBERED AND HELD IN OUR HEARTS ALWAYS. DOCTOR MORGAN, THANK YOU FOR CHECKING OUR LITTLE (NOW BIG) BOGEY THE CAT OVER SO THOROUGHLY AND GIVING US ADVICE ON THE RAISING OF THIS NEW LITTLE GUY. YOU ARE BOTH BEAUTIFUL, INSIDE AND OUT.

Dr. Carling Matejka

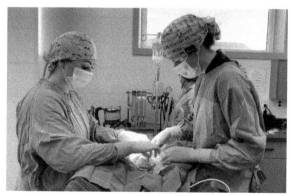

Doctors Matejka and Wiese

Dr. Morgan Wiese

SIMON'S HEAVENLY KITTY FRIENDS

George

Benny

Cheechoo

Sammy

Squeak

Buttons

Gatito

Ralph

Jade

GATITO

BENNY

CHEECHOO

SAMMY

SQUEAK

BUTTONS

GEORGE

RALPH

JADE

SIMON

SIMON'S HEAVENLY DOG FRIENDS

Maddy

Coby

Randy and Rudy

Jumbo

Keira

Mac

MADDY

COBY

RANDY

RUDY

JUMBO

KEIRA

SIMON THE CAT

MAC

THE FACES OF LOVE .....

**Bruce (Dad)
and Simon**

**Bruce (Dad)
and Bogey**

**M.R. (Mom)
and Simon**

**M.R. (Mom)
and Bogey**

**Millie
and Coby**

**Lisa
and Maddy**

**Lisa and John
and Lucy**

**Patty
and Simon**

**Joey
and Simon**

**Brenda
and Sammy**

**Kathy
and Buttons**

**Emerson
and Buttons**

**Debbie
and Blue**

**Debbie
and Goose**

**Debbie and
Opi and Lucy**

WHEN THE KITTY GOES, LOVE BECOMES A MEMORY,
THE MEMORY THEN BECOMES A TREASURE

OUR PETS ARE NOT OUR WHOLE LIFE BUT THEY MAKE OUR LIFE WHOLE

NO ONE CAN TRULY UNDERSTAND THE BOND FORMED WITH THE
CATS WE LOVE UNTIL THEY EXPERIENCE THE LOSS OF ONE

IF THE KINDEST SOULS WERE REWARDED WITH THE
LONGEST LIVES, DOGS WOULD OUTLIVE US ALL

WHAT A BEAUTIFUL WORLD IT WOULD BE IF
HUMANS HAD HEARTS LIKE DOGS

THE WORLD WOULD BE A NICE PLACE IF EVERYONE HAD THE
ABILITY TO LOVE AS UNCONDITIONALLY AS A DOG OR A CAT

WHAT GREATER GIFT THAN THE LOVE OF A DOG

WHAT GREATER GIFT THAN THE LOVE OF A CAT

CPSIA information can be obtained
at www.ICGtesting.com
Printed in the USA
BVHW051951070721
611297BV00001B/2

9 780228 854029